BLEAK HOUSE

CHARLES DICKENS

www.realreads.co.uk

Retold by Gill Tavner
Illustrated by Karen Donnelly

Published by Real Reads Ltd
Stroud, Gloucestershire, UK
www.realreads.co.uk

First published in 2007

ISBN 978-1-906230-04-3

Printed in China by Imago Ltd
Designed by Lucy Guenot
Typeset by Bookcraft Ltd, Stroud, Gloucestershire

CONTENTS

THE CHARACTERS

Mr Jarndyce

Mr Jarndyce becomes Esther's legal guardian. Can he keep her safe and happy in his home at Bleak House? Can he protect his young friends from the family curse?

Lady Dedlock

The proud and dignified wife of Sir Leicester Dedlock. Why does she make Esther's heart beat so violently? What secrets is she hiding? Why is she afraid of Tulkinghorn?

Esther Sommerson

As a child, Esther lived with her strict godmother. She has never experienced love or happiness. Will she find either at Bleak House?

Richard Carstone

Richard is a handsome, optimistic young man. Will he escape the grip of the Jarndyce curse?

Ada Clare

Ada is beautiful and trusting. Can she find happiness in spite of the Jarndyce curse?

Mr Tulkinghorn

Tulkinghorn is a cold, calculating lawyer who knows no mercy or pity. Can he gain power over Lady Dedlock by discovering her secrets?

Joe

Poor, orphaned Joe struggles to survive on the streets of London. What will happen to him when he becomes entangled in mysteries he doesn't understand?

BLEAK HOUSE

'It would have been far better, Esther, if you had never been born; far better if you had never had a birthday.'

Many children have happy birthdays, but not Esther. This was her twelfth, and they had always been like this. Esther knew that other children celebrated their birthdays, but as her godmother had never allowed her to accept a party invitation she wasn't sure how. She suspected it wasn't like this.

Poor Esther looked across the silent table at her godmother's stern face. 'Please tell me why I shouldn't have been born,' she asked, close to tears. 'Did my mother die giving birth to me? Did I do something to her?'

'Your mother, Esther, did not die. She is your disgrace, and you are hers. You must forget your mother. Now go to your room, and pray that you can be good enough to overcome the shadow of your birth.'

That was all Esther ever heard about her mother. She crept into bed and held her only friend, Little Dolly, close to her wet cheek.
'I do try to be kind, Dolly. I do try to be good-hearted. Why doesn't anyone love me?'

Two more birthdays passed before anything changed in Esther's lonely life. Shortly after her fourteenth birthday, her godmother fell seriously ill and died. Esther found herself being packed into a stagecoach by her godmother's witch-like servant, Mrs Rachel. Full of sadness for her loveless childhood and fear of an unknown future, Esther at first failed to notice the gentleman with whom she shared the coach.

'Come, come, little Esther. Why weep?'

Looking up, she took in his iron-grey hair and pleasant, gentle smile.

'Why couldn't they love me?' she sobbed.

'Why was Mrs Rachel so pleased to see me go?'

'Confound Mrs Rachel!' said the gentleman with a hint of anger. 'Let her fly away in a high wind on her broomstick.' This brought a smile to Esther's face.

'That's better,' the gentleman smiled back.

'Forgive me for asking, sir', she asked him, 'but who are you, and where are we going?'

He declined to tell her his name, but she learned that her godmother had asked him to look after her, and that he intended to do all he could to provide her with a happy life. Eventually they drew up outside a homely-looking school surrounded by trees. Her companion explained, 'Greenleaf is a first-rate educational establishment. Your education shall be completed here, and your future comfort secured.'

As they parted, Esther promised her guardian, 'I will be industrious, contented and true-hearted. I will do some good for someone and, if I can, win some love.'

'I know you will, dear Esther. I know you will.'

Esther was true to her word. Greenleaf was a small school, and she was soon loved by everybody there. A quick learner herself,

Esther was soon able to teach the younger
children. Homesick new youngsters were
assigned to Esther's care, where they received
gentle comfort and love. Each year, her fellow
pupils made simple birthday presents for their
beloved Esther, and as each birthday passed
she grew more accustomed to the special tea

party and the loving wishes. Nobody's presence in a school could have been more valuable than Esther's; nobody's absence more dreaded.

But Esther could not stay at school for ever, and eventually the time came for her to leave. Her twentieth birthday was celebrated with an air of sadness. The younger children clung to her and cried. Waving goodbye from her coach window, Esther felt pleased that she had remained true to her word. Not only had she given love, she had won some for herself too. She wiped away her tears, and wondered what lay ahead.

In London the fog was everywhere. Fog up the Thames, where it flowed through the dirtiest, darkest places Esther had ever seen; fog down

the Thames, where it rolled past the smoke-billowing ships and waterside factories. Fog surrounded the busy, ill-tempered people as they jostled their way through the streets; fog got into the eyes and lungs of old men and tiny babies, making them cough and spit up blood.

It was dirty fog, sooty fog, so thick that the gas lamps glowed orange even in the daytime. The dense fog grew denser, the muddy streets muddier, and the people more ill-tempered as Esther's coach entered the city's legal district and stopped in a small courtyard.

'Is there a fire somewhere?' Esther asked a passer-by.

'Oh no, miss. This fog is a feature of London.'

Esther coughed as she entered the building, and was still wiping soot from her eyes when she was introduced to two young people. 'Miss Ada, Mr Carstone,' said the lawyer's clerk, 'this is Miss Esther Sommerson.'

Ada, seventeen years old with soft blue eyes and a smiling face, timidly shook Esther's hand. Esther liked her immediately. Ada's younger cousin, Richard Carstone, was just as cheerful and pleasant. Though she liked the pair, Esther still had no idea why she had been brought here to this lawyer's office in grimy London.

The clerk explained. 'Miss Sommerson, your guardian has chosen you to be a companion to Miss Ada Clare.' Esther and Ada smiled at each other. 'Miss Ada and Mr Carstone are the wards in Jarndyce and Jarndyce.'

Noticing Esther's puzzled look, Richard laughed. 'You've never heard of Jarndyce and Jarndyce, have you?' Esther shook her head.

Inviting Esther to take a seat between himself and his cousin, Richard explained. 'Jarndyce and Jarndyce is a legal battle which has been occupying the courts for years. It is about an inheritance, but the lawyers are making hard work of it. This London fog is in their brains and in their courtrooms. Nobody can see their way through it. Our future comfort depends upon the outcome of Jarndyce and Jarndyce. Until the case is settled, Ada and I are the wards of our distant cousin, Mr John Jarndyce.'

'Mr Jarndyce?' repeated Esther. 'I have never heard of Mr Jarndyce.'

'We will all meet him tomorrow. The three of us are to live with him at his home, Bleak House, until the lawyers reach their conclusion in the case of Jarndyce and Jarndyce.'

From London fog to Bleak House – in
spite of her companions' cheerfulness, Esther
wondered how happy they could all be in a
home with such a name.

Bleak House, however, defied its
name wonderfully. Greenery clambered
enthusiastically up its cosy walls, sunlight
bounced joyfully from every window, and
a melodic fanfare of birdsong accompanied
their coach as it rattled up the drive.

Mr John Jarndyce strode towards them, arms outstretched, his silvery hair reflecting the sunlight and his smile assuring them of a warm welcome. Esther recognised him as the man who had rescued her from the witch, the guardian who had sent her to Greenleaf School where she had been so happy.

'Ada, Esther, Rick. Welcome to your new home.'

Esther stared at him. She wanted to thank him for creating so much happiness in her orphaned life.

Mr Jarndyce saw the gratitude in her face. 'Do not thank me, Esther. Let the past be taken for granted. If anybody thanks me too much I have to run away immediately and hide! Now, let me show you to your rooms. Who would like a cup of tea?'

An hour later, a shaft of sunlight warming his back, John Jarndyce placed his empty cup on his saucer. Richard had asked him a difficult question, and he answered it very carefully. 'My dear Rick, we must never have high hopes of Jarndyce and Jarndyce. The lawyers have twisted it to such a state of confusion that the only ones that will benefit from it are themselves. *They* may end up rich, but nobody else will. It is a constant  cycle of interrogating, filing, cross-filing, arguing, sealing and reporting. It has already ruined the lives of many innocent people who should have benefited from it. My own uncle, who owned this house before me, named it Bleak House when he gave up all hope of gaining anything from the case. He shot himself.'

He paused and looked seriously at Richard. 'Rick, you must live as though you had never heard of Jarndyce and Jarndyce. If you set any hope by it, it will be your ruin.'

Many miles away, in an old, cold and echoing home, Jarndyce and Jarndyce was also on people's lips. Sir Leicester Dedlock was reading determinedly through a pile of documents with his lawyer. Lady Dedlock sat in the window seat, half listening but thoroughly bored. Her beautiful face lacked radiance as her sad eyes looked out at the gentle rain that always seemed to fall at Chesney Wold.

'Pray, Mr Tulkinghorn,' she said, rising slowly and walking languidly towards the lawyer, 'how long does it take to talk of one day's progress in the case of Jarndyce and Jarndyce?'

'My dear Lady Dedlock, it is a case confounding the most brilliant legal minds. It is a case ... Lady Dedlock ... ?'

Wondering why the lawyer had stopped, Sir
Leicester looked up. His wife was trembling,
staring at the sheet of paper Tulkinghorn held
in his hand.

'Whose is that handwriting?' she whispered.

'Oh, just some legal scribe,' replied
Tulkinghorn, his sharp grey eyes watching her
carefully. 'Why do you ask?'

Lady Dedlock struggled to regain her
composure. Holding the back of Tulkinghorn's
chair, she repeated quietly, 'That
writing, that writing ... '
Sir Leicester was not fast
enough to catch his wife
as she fell, faint,
to the floor.

Once he had returned to London, Mr Tulkinghorn pushed the document in which Lady Dedlock had shown such interest under the nose of his office clerk. The lawyer's piercing eyes were intimidating. He repeated his question, 'Who was the legal scribe who prepared this document?'

'All I know, sir, is that he called himself Nemo.'

'Nemo? Don't you know that Nemo is the Latin word for "nobody"?' Tulkinghorn's expressionless face revealed none of the frustration he was feeling. He was a man of many secrets, and an expert in concealing them. 'Show me where this Nemo character lives.'

'I don't know where he lives, sir, but I have seen him talking to a young boy in the street.'

'Take me to the boy. Now.'

Tulkinghorn's black clothes gave him the appearance of death's shadow as he strode through the squalid streets which the poorest of Londoners called home. His face remained inscrutable, showing neither disgust nor pity. He looked only straight ahead, ignoring the lives wasting away as he passed by.

'Here's the boy, sir.'

A very muddy, very thin, very ragged boy shrank back as Tulkinghorn loomed over him.

'Your name, boy?'

'Joe, sir. I haven't done nuffink.'

'Tell me about Nemo.'

'I know nuffink 'cept that he is very good to me. Days when he has any money, he gives me some. When he has no money, he sits wiv me and says "I am as poor as you today, Joe." He's my only friend.'

'Show me where he lives, and I'll give you some money.'

Five minutes later, Tulkinghorn and Joe stood on opposite sides of a bed in a dirty room. Lying very still upon the bed was a ragged, neglected, unkempt man of about forty.

'God help us!' exclaimed Joe, 'Nemo's dead!'

The lonely figure on the bed was indeed dead. Joe stared at his friend as Tulkinghorn searched through the man's clothes. Joe thought he saw Tulkinghorn's swift hand removing a piece of paper from a

coat pocket and slipping it into his own. But Tulkinghorn, who wished to appear dissatisfied with his search, complained that all he had found was evidence that Nemo had taken too much opium.

Leaving as purposefully as he had arrived, Tulkinghorn left Joe alone with the body of his friend. 'He wos very good to me,' muttered Joe to himself. 'He wos very good to me.'

Away from the fog and squalor of London, the new inhabitants of Bleak House had passed several sunny months. Firm friendships were developing between the three young people, and their love and respect for Mr Jarndyce grew daily. Esther was honoured to be given responsibility for managing all the household affairs. She was pleased that Mr Jarndyce sought and respected her opinion about so many things. She was flattered that both Richard and Ada chose to confide in her.

Although Esther had never seen two people falling in love before, she understood the meaning of Ada's increasingly shy blushes, and noticed that Richard's restless energy was softened by gentleness in Ada's presence. She was not at all surprised when Ada, aglow with joy and pride, approached her one sunny morning. 'Esther, I need to talk to you. I think you should sit down.'

Smiling, Esther obliged. Ada sat next to her
and held her hands. 'Oh, Esther. Richard says
that he loves me dearly.'

Esther put a loving arm around Ada's
shoulders. 'My dear Ada, I know he does, and
I am truly happy for you both. We must tell Mr
Jarndyce.'

That evening, they had a guest at the supper table. Intelligent and handsome, Allan Woodcourt was a doctor and a new friend of Mr Jarndyce. Richard talked with enthusiastic openness about his future with Ada. 'Of course, we will not marry for several years.'

Mr Jarndyce nodded and smiled. 'Very wise, Rick. You must establish yourself in a profession before you can hope to support a family.'

'Oh, I will. I've thought about joining the army. Or perhaps I could be a surgeon.'

'Slow down, Rick,' laughed Mr Jarndyce, enjoying the young man's excitement. The evening sun shone into the room as the older man continued, 'I have connections in both the army and in medicine who could help you to advance quickly.' He smiled knowingly at Dr Woodcourt. 'First, however, you must decide which career to commit yourself to. You cannot do everything!'

'Maybe I won't have to do either. If Jarndyce and Jarndyce can make us rich … '

'Rick! Rick!' Mr Jarndyce stood up suddenly, his face drained of colour. 'You must not build up your expectations based on the family curse. It will surely ruin you as it ruined my uncle.'

The evening sun slipped behind a cloud. Ada rested her hand on Richard's arm and said softly, 'We should forget about Jarndyce and Jarndyce. It will only make us unhappy.'

As Mr Jarndyce sat down again, Esther noticed his hands trembling.

'Don't worry,' said Richard, meeting Mr Jarndyce's concerned look with a reassuring smile. 'Maybe the law is the profession for me. Then I would be able to understand Jarndyce and Jarndyce. I would be able to make sure that everything is done properly, and look after all our interests.'

Mr Jarndyce finished his supper in silence. To ease the atmosphere, Esther engaged Allan Woodcourt in polite conversation. When Ada teased her about Dr Woodcourt the next day, Esther was surprised to find herself blushing.

The next evening, Mr Jarndyce entertained other guests. Sir Leicester and Lady Dedlock were making a rare visit to their old family friend on their way home from their London residence. Normally so magnificent and proud, Lady Dedlock seemed to be suffering from a weariness of soul, and took little interest in the people around her.

When dinner was served, Lady Dedlock took her seat opposite Esther. Esther suddenly gasped. Her heart thumped rapidly. She tried to compose herself, but felt flustered and troubled. When Lady Dedlock's eyes met hers, they seemed for a second to spring out of their languor and hold her gaze. Lady Dedlock's face flushed. For a split second, she too seemed flustered.

Esther felt confused by her inexplicable feeling of discomfort in Lady Dedlock's presence. Looking at Lady Dedlock gave Esther the strange sensation that she was looking at herself through a broken mirror.

For Lady Dedlock, this visit to their old friend Mr Jarndyce at Bleak House was a welcome end to a difficult week. She was happy to delay her return to the dreariness of Chesney Wold, and very happy to be a long way from Mr Tulkinghorn. She supposed that her own strange reaction to Esther must simply be a result of her tiredness and troubled mind.

Lady Dedlock was beginning to distrust Tulkinghorn. He had been watching her very carefully since she had asked about the handwriting. She regretted that now. Earlier that week, Tulkinghorn's eyes had seemed particularly searching when he told her the identity of the legal scribe.

'He is called Nemo,' he had told her. 'I have seen him.' Aware of being closely observed, Lady Dedlock had feigned indifference. 'He was dead.' The lawyer peered over his spectacles.

'How very shocking.'

'Shocking indeed, Lady Dedlock. He had

no one to tend him but a filthy street urchin called Joe.'

'How sad.'

'Sad indeed, Lady Dedlock. Sad indeed.'

That very night, Lady Dedlock had dressed in her maid's clothes and walked alone through the London streets. Although dressed as a servant, it was clear to anybody that she was not

accustomed to the dirt and choking fog. The tumbling, decaying buildings between which she walked were swarming with misery; misery that powerful and wealthy people like her husband could and should have relieved, but chose to ignore.

People stared after her as she searched for a filthy street urchin called Joe. She found him where he was so often to be found, sweeping the road in the hope of a few pennies being thrown his way.

'Come here, boy.' Joe obediently did what he was asked.

'Did you know Nemo?'

Joe nodded, 'Why, did you know him too?'

'Of course I didn't,' Lady Dedlock snapped at him before remembering that she needed the help of this grubby boy. She recollected herself. 'Can you take me to where he worked, where he lived, where he died, where he is buried?'

'I know nuffink, missis.'

'You must show me these dreadful places. Please don't speak to me; just do what I ask and I will pay you well.

In the early hours of the morning, at the gate of the paupers' graveyard, Lady Dedlock opened her purse to give Joe a gold sovereign. He noticed how soft and white her hand was, and how the jewels on her rings sparkled. 'Funny kind of servant you are,' he said as he disappeared into the darkness.

Lady Dedlock fell to her knees and wept.

The ever-devious Tulkinghorn had been making enquiries of his own. Using a private detective, he had gained possession of a number of other documents in the same handwriting – documents with signatures. Nemo now had an identity. Tulkinghorn had learned that before his fortunes changed and he ended up in such misery, Nemo was known as Captain Hawden. To gain real power over Lady Dedlock, Tulkinghorn now had to find out why Captain Hawden appeared to be of such significance to Lady Dedlock.

Poor little Joe lived in this world, but had very little understanding of it, and he was bewildered by the attention he had received since Nemo's death. He was regularly summoned to Tulkinghorn's office. At one meeting a third person was present, a woman with a disturbingly witch-like look. She was introduced as Mrs Rachel Chadbrand.

'Mrs Rachel,' began Tulkinghorn, 'I believe you know the name Hawden.'

'Indeed I do. I used to work for a very stern, very secretive lady.'

Tulkinghorn looked approving. 'Go on.'

'This lady looked after a little girl called Esther, who she said was her god-daughter. On one occasion, and I do believe it slipped out by accident, she told me that the little girl's real surname was Hawden. I had always known her as Sommerson, Esther Sommerson.'

Even Tulkinghorn, so full of secrets himself, gasped. Miss Esther Sommerson of Bleak House, Mr Jarndyce's ward, was possibly Nemo's daughter?

The lawyer turned his attention to Joe. 'You say someone was asking about Nemo?'

'Yes. She wos a lady as sed she wos a servant. She wanted to see the berryin' ground wot he's berried in.'

'Describe her.'

Joe did as he was asked and then, no longer useful, he was dismissed with a few coins. He went to sit beside the magnificence of St Paul's Cathedral. 'Move on, boy, you're dirtying the place,' said a constable.

Joe felt tired, weak and feverish. 'I'm always a-movin' on,' he muttered, 'I've been a-movin' ever since I wos born. Where can I possibly move to?'

The question had no answer. The hundreds of starving children on London's streets just had to keep a-movin' on.

Richard was away in London, and Bleak House was not the happy place it had been. Mr Jarndyce, Esther, and especially Ada, missed his cheerful presence. Against all advice, and ignoring their pleas, Richard had moved to London to pursue the case of Jarndyce and Jarndyce. Dr Woodcourt, who often visited London, promised to befriend Richard, and he became a regular visitor to Bleak House, bringing news and letters from Richard. Esther always looked forward to his visits.

Richard's letters to Mr Jarndyce became increasingly cold, haughty and resentful. He accused his generous guardian of being dishonest, of working against him. 'We must not blame Rick,' Mr Jarndyce told Esther, 'His blood is infected with the poison of the case. I have seen many fine, fresh hearts poisoned by Jarndyce and Jarndyce. We must be patient with Rick, and hope – for his sake – that he sees sense before it is too late.'

'And for poor Ada's sake,' added Esther.

Mr Jarndyce nodded, looking up at Esther with concern. 'My dear,' he said, 'you are shivering, and you look very pale. Are you unwell?'

Esther was far from well. The dreaded smallpox had found Bleak House and knocked on its door, and Esther fell victim to its malicious presence. The next day she lay in bed with a high fever, then a livid rash spread across her face and body. Dr Woodcourt became a kind, helpful and increasingly loving friend. He visited her every day, and when her rash began to form into hard red lumps that she wanted to scratch, he told her severely to leave them alone.

Tulkinghorn bided his time. He thought he could use his newly-discovered secret to gain power over Lady Dedlock, but it would not be easy to accomplish. One evening at Chesney Wold, when Sir Leicester had left the room to search for some papers, Tulkinghorn found his moment.

Sitting in a shaft of cold, grey moonlight, he looked his quarry in the eye. 'Lady Dedlock, have you ever noticed that Miss Sommerson looks rather like you, and rather like your old friend Captain Hawden?'

'Miss Sommerson of Bleak House?' She sat motionless for a moment, then looked away.

The observant Tulkinghorn noticed a tremor pass over her. He knew that she had understood what he was suggesting. Admiring Lady Dedlock's self-control and dignity, Tulkinghorn continued. 'I have not decided what use I shall make of your secret, but for now it will remain between us.' Tulkinghorn stood up, as if to assert his new power. 'After all, we would not want your husband to hear about this, would we?'

Lady Dedlock remained in her seat as Tulkinghorn left the room. As the door closed, she buried her face in her hands. 'Oh, my child! Not dead at birth as my cruel sister told me, but secretly – and no doubt sternly – raised by her! Oh, my poor Esther!'

Bleak House had been very bleak for several weeks. Alone in her room, Esther fought a desperate battle with her illness. Finally it was defeated, but the retreating disease left Esther's beautiful face disfigured with the marks of its presence.

Looking at her new appearance in her mirror, Esther told herself that it didn't matter. She knew that Mr Jarndyce and Ada would still love her, but she sadly gave up any hopes she might have had relating to Allan Woodcourt. Arranging her hair tidily, she left her room for the first time in weeks, and went to join her friends.

'My dear, dear girl,' cried Mr Jarndyce with joy as he and Ada wrapped their arms around their beloved Esther. Tears of relief that Esther had been spared flowed freely down their cheeks.

Whilst Esther was fighting the fevered grip of disease, Lady Dedlock was feeling the tightening of Tulkinghorn's icy grip. Desperate to spare her husband the heartache of discovering the truth, and no longer able to live with Tulkinghorn's threats, she reached a difficult decision. First, however, there was something she had to do.

Lady Dedlock found Esther in the woods below Bleak House. Esther was surprised by Lady Dedlock's footsteps, but that did not fully explain the wild beating of her heart. As she looked up at Lady Dedlock's face, she saw something that she had longed for as a child.

It was the look that only a mother can give a daughter.

Lady Dedlock fell to her knees and pulled Esther to her. 'Esther,' she cried, 'I am your wretched, unhappy mother. I thought you were dead. Please try to forgive me.'

Esther returned the embrace, her heart overflowing with a daughter's natural love. 'Oh mother, of course I forgive you.'

Together they wept over their lost years. From her mother's lips, Esther learned who she really was, and understood the circumstances of her birth. Eventually, Lady Dedlock sighed sadly as she reluctantly stood up to leave. 'Oh, Esther. This is our first and last time together. This must forever be our secret. Should we meet again we must be strangers, but whatever you might hear about me in the future, remember that your mother loves you.'

Esther watched her mother's dignified back, shaking with sobs, disappear into the shadows. She was certain that she would never see her again.

Dr Woodcourt was worried about Richard. He insisted that Esther, Mr Jarndyce and Ada should travel with him to London to visit their friend and cousin. He assured Mr Jarndyce that Richard's hostility towards him had now passed.

Richard was lying on an infested mattress in a dirty, damp room. Ada rushed to his side. As the others followed, he struggled to sit up, void of his youthful joy and energy.

The truth came out. The long-running case of Jarndyce and Jarndyce had finally been decided in Richard's favour. He should have been a rich man, but Mr Jarndyce was right. The lawyers had drawn out the case just long enough to ensure that all of the wealth in the

contested will had been used to cover their
costs. They had all patted their pockets and
Richard, to whom the wealth should have
passed, received nothing.

Meanwhile Richard, with little money to
spend on comforts, had neglected his health,
until disease struck him down. Now, his hope

destroyed, he looked into Ada's tearful eyes.
'My love,' he whispered with his last breath,
'I am so sorry.'

Returning to the gentle beauty of Bleak House
offered some comfort to Esther, Mr Jarndyce,
Ada and Allan Woodcourt. One evening, as
the orange glow of the descending winter sun
warmed the room, Mr Jarndyce asked Esther to
join him in a stroll.

Looking at his warm smile, Esther felt that
she had never felt such thankfulness in her
heart. She tried to express her gratitude, but
Mr Jarndyce silenced her. 'You have done me
a world of good, Esther. You have brought joy
and light into Bleak House and into my life. You
must believe that, whatever your answer to my
next question might be, you will gain nothing
in my heart by accepting and lose nothing by
rejecting. My love for you will remain unaltered.'

Sure that she knew what the question would be, Esther felt grateful for this opportunity to make him happy. She tried to ignore the sense of loss she felt as her thoughts flickered briefly to Allan Woodcourt.

'Next month,' said Mr Jarndyce, looking into Esther's eyes, 'I hope to take the happiest and best step of my life. I should like to walk with you down the aisle. I should like to give your hand in marriage to the thoroughly good Allan Woodcourt.'

'Dr Woodcourt?' Esther's legs felt weak.

'He has asked for the honour of your hand. Will you accept?'

Tears of joy rolled down Esther's disease-marked cheeks as she looked up at her fatherly guardian. He gently turned her around to see Allan walking nervously towards them.

That same evening, while the inhabitants of Bleak House made plans for a wedding and a bright future, a lady – pale, thin and exhausted – knelt beside an unmarked grave in London's paupers' graveyard.

After saying goodbye to Esther in the woods, Lady Dedlock had left her home and her riches, and disappeared amongst London's poor. Dressed in servants' clothes, she had walked the streets for weeks, living like Joe on scraps of food and charity. Whether her decision was courageous or cowardly, she neither knew nor cared.

Her terror of Tulkinghorn, her guilt, her great shame, and her mourning for a little girl's lost childhood gnawed away at her soul, while the cold, the wind, and the rain gnawed at her body. This proud lady, now just another nobody, rested upon the grave of a man she had once loved.

Her finger, once so soft and white, traced the name 'Nemo' into the soil. Her final words, 'Our daughter, our daughter,' floated away on the wind.

Nobody heard. Nobody was there when she died.

TAKING THINGS FURTHER

The real read

This *Real Reads* version of *Bleak House* is a retelling of Charles Dickens' magnificent work. If you would like to read the full novel in all its original splendour, many complete editions are available, from bargain paperbacks to beautifully-bound hardbacks. You may well find a copy in your local charity shop.

Filling in the spaces

The loss of so many of Charles Dickens' original words is a sad but necessary part of the shortening process. We have had to make some difficult decisions, omitting subplots and details, some important, some less so, but all interesting. We have also, at times, taken the liberty of combining two events into one, or of giving a character words or actions that originally belong to another. The points below will fill in some of the gaps, but nothing can beat the original.

- Esther's godmother, who is really her aunt, has arranged for Mr John Jarndyce to become Esther's legal guardian upon her aunt's death.

- The legal firm of Kenge and Carboy's is supposed to be looking after the interests of Richard and Ada in the Jarndyce and Jarndyce case.

- Dickens story includes a family called the Jellbys. He uses Mrs Jellby to highlight a social problem that he names 'telescopic misanthropy' – she is so concerned about the welfare of poor people in Africa that she neglects her own family. Her daughter Caddy becomes a great friend of Esther, and eventually marries a dancer called Prince Turveydrop.

- Nemo's room is rented from a dishonest man appropriately called Krooks. Krooks dies of spontaneous combustion – burning up completely for no apparent reason – which Dickens believed was possible.

- Another character, Miss Flight, watches life pass her by as she follows the case of Jarndyce and Jarndyce.

- Tulkinghorn uses Lady Dedlock's French maid, Hortense, to help Joe identify Lady Dedlock. Hortense eventually gets so angry with Tulkinghorn that she shoots and kills him.

- Lady Dedlock is amongst the suspects for Tulkinghorn's murder. This is another reason for her to run away.

- When Esther was born illegitimately, her aunt told her mother that she was stillborn. Her aunt then gave up her own chance of happy marriage in order to raise Esther.

- Richard's period of indecision about what profession to enter is much longer than in this version. His indecision is blamed upon the uncertainty of the case of Jarndyce and Jarndyce. He secretly marries Ada, who is expecting his child when he dies.

- Esther and her maid nurse Joe through smallpox before both catching it themselves.

- The process by which secrets are gradually revealed is simplified in this version. Dickens allows a young lawyer called Guppy and a private detective called Mr Bucket to discover much of the truth.

- Lady Dedlock dies unaware that her husband has forgiven her, and that she has been cleared of Tulkinghorn's murder.

- The process by which Nemo is identified is considerably more complex than in this version.

- Mr Jarndyce proposes to Esther and she accepts. He releases her from the engagement so that she can marry Woodcourt. Mr Jarndyce buys them a house called Little Bleak House. They live happily and have two children. Ada and her child live happily in Bleak House with Mr Jarndyce.

Back in time

Victorian England was a period of great transition. Many people left their traditional rural lives to seek work and wealth in London. The population of Victorian London therefore increased rapidly. Many, like Joe, were living in terrible poverty. This was a cause of great concern to many people.

The legal profession had great responsibilities, but faced much criticism. In *Bleak House* Dickens shows greedy lawyers becoming rich whilst ruining other people's lives. Dickens based 'Jarndyce and Jarndyce' on a real legal case, which lasted for fifty-three years. As his own father had been imprisoned for debt, Dickens was particularly critical of the legal system.

Queen Victoria represented all that the ideal Victorian woman should be. Women's responsibility was to maintain domestic stability through marriage, family values and motherhood. Having children outside marriage – as Lady Dedlock had Esther – brought great disgrace upon both mother and child.

Smallpox was greatly feared – even today the World Health Organisation calls it 'one of the most devastating diseases known to humanity'. In the eighteenth century, smallpox killed a third of its victims, blinded many, and left most with deep scars on their faces – like Esther's. During Victoria's reign a vaccine was developed which a century later eventually eradicated the disease.

Finding out more

We recommend the following books and websites to gain a greater understanding of Charles Dickens' and Esther's England.

Books

- Terry Deary, *Loathsome London* (Horrible Histories), Scholastic, 2005.

- Terry Deary, *Vile Victorians* (Horrible Histories), Scholastic, 1994.

- *Victorian London*, Watling Street Publishing, 2005.

- Ann Kramer, *Victorians* (Eyewitness Guides), Dorling Kindersley, 1998.

- Mandy Ross, *Victorian Schools* (Life in the Past), Heinemann, 2005.

- Peter Ackroyd, *Dickens*, BBC, 2003.

Websites

- www.victorianweb.org
Scholarly information about all aspects of Victorian life, including literature and culture.

- www.bbc.co.uk/history/british/victorians.
The BBC's interactive site about Victorian Britain, with a wide range of information and activities for all ages.

- www.dickensmuseum.com
Home of the Dickens Museum in London, with details about exhibits, events and helpful links.

- www.dickensworld.co.uk
Dickens World, based in Chatham in Kent, is a themed visitor complex featuring the life, books and times of Charles Dickens.

- www.bbc.co.uk/history/trail/victorian_britain

A site offering source materials and guidance in how to use them, as well as a wealth of information. It contains a section on using *Bleak House* as source material.

Food for thought

Here are some things to think about if you are reading *Bleak House* alone, or ideas for discussion if you are reading it with friends.

In retelling *Bleak House* we have tried to recreate, as accurately as possible, Dickens' original plot and characters. We have also tried to imitate aspects of his style. Remember, however, that this is not the original work; thinking about the points below, therefore, can help you begin to understand Charles Dickens' craft. To move forward from here, turn to the full-length version of *Bleak House* and lose yourself in his wonderful storytelling.

Starting points

- Which character interests you the most? Why?

- Why do you think Mr Jarndyce warns Richard about the Jarndyce and Jarndyce legal case?

- What clues does Dickens give us that Tulkinghorn is an unpleasant man?

- How surprised were you to discover the relationships between Nemo, Lady Dedlock and Esther?

- How do you feel towards Joe?

Themes

What do you think Charles Dickens is saying about the following themes in *Bleak House*?

- the legal profession

- poverty

- illness

- secrets

- love

Style

Can you find paragraphs containing examples of the following?

- descriptions of setting and atmosphere

- the use of repetition to enhance description

- different characters speaking in different ways

- the use of imagery, alliteration or assonance to enhance description

Look closely at how these paragraphs are written. What do you notice? Can you write a paragraph in the same style?

Symbols

Writers frequently use symbols in their work to deepen the reader's emotions and understanding. Think about how the symbols in this list match the action in *Bleak House*.

- fog

- hands

- light and shadow

- city and countryside